VIVA ZAPATA

To the children all over the world who don't have enough to eat — like the 50% of children in Guatemala who suffer from chronic malnutrition — and to all those who work for deep change — E.S. & M.K.T.

For Emiliano Francisco Arteage — S.C.

Published in 2009 in Canada and Great Britain by Tradewind Books
Text copyright © 2009 by Emilie Smith and Margarita Kenefic Tejada   Illustrations copyright © 2009 by Stefan Czernecki.

Book & cover design by Tim Rhodes   Scanning by Disc

Printed and bound in Canada on 100% ancient forest-friendly paper certified by the Forest Stewardship Council (FSC)

2 4 6 8 10 9 7 5 3 1

The publisher acknowledges the support of the Canada Council for the Arts. The publisher also wishes to thank the Government of British Columbia for the financial support it has extended through the book publishing tax credit program and the British Columbia Arts Council. The publisher acknowledges the financial support of the Government of Canada through the Book Publishing Industry Development Program (BPIDP) and the Association for the Export of Canadian Books (AECB) for our publishing program.

Cataloguing-in-Publication Data for this book is available from The British Library.

Library and Archives Canada Cataloguing in Publication

Smith, Emilie, 1963-
    Viva Zapata / Emilie Smith and Margarita Kenefic Tejada ; illustrated by
Stefan Czernecki.

ISBN 978-1-896580-55-5

    1. Zapata, Emiliano, 1879-1919--Juvenile fiction.
I. Czernecki, Stefan, 1946- II. Tejada, Margarita Kenefic, 1954-
III. Title.

PS8637.M5622 V59 2009   jC813'.6   C2009-900915-3

Canada

Canada Council for the Arts   Conseil des Arts du Canada

BRITISH COLUMBIA ARTS COUNCIL
We acknowledge the support of the Province of British Columbia through the British Columbia Arts Council

FSC   Mixed So
Cert no. SW-COC-0
© 1996 FSC

VIVA ZAPATA

By Emilie Smith and Margarita Kenefic Tejada

Illustrated by Stefan Czernecki

TRADEWIND BOOKS

Vancouver London

On the morning of Emiliano's seventh birthday, the old mare Lucita gave birth to her last foal.

"He's black like a shadow," said Emiliano. "I'll call him Sombra."

Sombra grew strong and feisty under Emiliano's care.

One day, Emiliano and Sombra rode far into the countryside, past tumbledown villages. None of the children waved as they galloped by.

Back home, Emiliano asked his mother, "Why are the children unhappy?"

"They don't have enough to eat," she replied.

"Why don't the farmers grow more corn?"

"Because they don't have enough land. That's just the way the world is," she answered.

But why is that the way the world is? Emiliano thought.

On the night before Emiliano's tenth birthday, a gang of bandidos crept into the stable and stole all the horses.

Except Lucita.

"She's too old. She'll slow us down," sneered Bad Carlos, their leader.

The next morning, a search party assembled to catch the bandidos.

"I want to come with you!" Emiliano said.

"You're too little," replied his father.

Emiliano rushed to the stable and threw his arms around Lucita.

"Papa won't let me go with him. We'll find Sombra ourselves."

All day Emiliano and Lucita rode, and late into the evening. They climbed the foothills of the Popocatepetl volcano until they saw a campfire. Bandidos snored in heaps all around. The stolen horses whinnied quietly nearby.

"Sombra!"

Emiliano jumped off Lucita and untied Sombra. Then he marched right up to the fire.

"I am Emiliano Zapata. This is my horse, Sombra. We're going home."

The bandidos, startled from their sleep, sat up and rubbed their eyes.

"Why, it's just a boy!" Bad Carlos exclaimed.

Just then Sombra snatched Bad Carlos' hat and Fat Chepe burst into laughter.

"Why are you laughing?" snarled Bad Carlos, shooting his pistol into the air. "Bandidos don't laugh!"

"Because I've never had so much fun," Fat Chepe answered, still laughing.

"Okay, little hombre," growled Bad Carlos. "Make all of us laugh and you can take your pony and go."

Emiliano and Sombra performed all sorts of tricks.

But not one of the bandidos laughed.
Fat Chepe spat into a grimy cup.
Bad Carlos picked at his teeth with a knife.
Things were looking grim.

"Why are you all so mean?" Emiliano asked.

"Because we never had enough tortillas to eat when we were little," said Bad Carlos.

"When I grow up," replied Emiliano, "I will help farmers get the land they need to grow food. No one will go hungry. And no one will need to become a bandido."

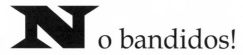o bandidos!

The crickets stopped singing. The coyotes in the hills stopped howling.

And the bandidos laughed and laughed—every last one of them. They laughed so hard they split their pants.

They were having so much fun they didn't notice Emiliano, Lucita and Sombra sneak away, taking with them all the stolen horses.

High above, the moon smiled, lighting the way. She knew. For Emiliano Zapata, this was only the beginning.

Emilie Smith was born in Argentina and lives in Vancouver, BC. She wrote this story with her friend Margarita Kenefic Tejada, who lives in Guatemala. They met many years ago when they both were living in a Mexican village about a day's horseback ride from Emiliano's home. Over the years these two friends have engaged in numerous acts of poetry and compassion.

Stefan Czernecki is one of North America's most respected illustrators. He lives in Vancouver, BC, but has a special place in his heart for Mexico. Several of his books have been translated into Spanish for Mexican children.

Emiliano Zapata was born in 1879 in a small town in the state of Morelos. His family was humble but independent, and his parents taught him to work hard in his own fields. The family raised many animals and Emiliano especially loved horses. He was orphaned at 16, but managed to support himself and get by. As a young man he became an advisor for the poor people in the countryside against the big landowners. Emiliano was modestly educated, but he was wise and courageous. In 1910, a great movement of Mexicans began to fight for the rights of the poor, and Emiliano Zapata became the leader of what was to become the Mexican Revolution—changing the face the country forever. Sadly, Emiliano was caught in an ambush and killed in 1919, but people around the world to this day admire his love for justice and freedom.